The SILVER SLIPPERS

Story and Pictures

by

Elizabeth Koda-Callan

WORKMAN PUBLISHING, NEW YORK

Library of Congress Cataloging-in-Publication Data

Koda-Callan, Elizabeth.
The silver slippers.

Summary: A young girl seems to be always out of step
in following her dream to become a prima ballerina,
until her mother's gift of a charm gives her the
confidence to keep going.
(1. Ballet dancing—Fiction. 2. Self-confidence—
Fiction) I. Title
PZ.K8175Si 1989   (E)   89-40370
ISBN 0-89480-618-1

Workman books are available at special discounts
when purchased in bulk for premiums and sales
promotions as well as for fund-raising or educational
use. Special editions or book excerpts can also be
created to specification. For details, contact the
Special Sales Director at the address below.

Workman Publishing Company
708 Broadway
New York, New York 10003

Printed in Hong Kong

First Printing October 1989

20 19 18 17 16 15 14 13 12 11

For Jane, Jennifer, Sara,
Chase and Lauren M.

Once there was a little girl who dreamed of being a ballerina. She longed for a day when she would dance on stage before a large audience. But until that day came she danced before a small one.

Twice a week the little girl took ballet lessons after school. She practiced at class and she practiced at home.

Ballet posters on the walls of her room inspired her. But no matter how hard she tried, she never could get into exactly the same position as the one that was on the poster.

In class she was never quite in step.

The little girl was frequently discouraged.

One day the teacher told the class that there was to be a ballet recital. "I haven't decided who will be the prima ballerina and lead the other dancers," she said.

"The prima ballerina!" thought the little girl. "I would really like to be the prima ballerina." But then she remembered her last practice session at the barre. "Oh, I could never be the prima ballerina, not the way I dance now," she thought.

That afternoon the little girl hurried home and told her mother about the ballet recital. She told her about her longing to be a star ballerina. "I think you can do it," said her mother. "You just have to practice—maybe even a bit more than the other girls. You have to decide what you want."

The little girl thought about what her mother had said. She decided that she really did want to be the prima ballerina.

The next day, while the little girl was practicing, her mother came into the room. "I have something for you," she said. She handed the little girl a small white box that was tied with a beautiful silver bow. The little girl untied the bow and opened the box. There, resting on a small cushion of velvet, was a pair of tiny silver slippers on a silver chain. "These slippers are special," said the little girl's mother. "They will help you become the prima ballerina by reminding you of what you want."

The little girl put on the necklace and looked in the mirror. The silver slippers glistened in the light. She wondered how a necklace could help her become the prima ballerina.

For the next few weeks, the little girl worked very hard. Every spare moment, she practiced. When her friends played outside, she practiced. When they went to the movies, she practiced. And all the time she practiced, she wore the silver slippers.

Days went by, and the little girl
danced better.

Weeks passed, and the little girl
continued to improve.

The teacher saw how hard the little girl had practiced and how much better she was dancing. When it was time to choose the lead dancer, the teacher chose the little girl!

The little girl rushed home after class to tell her mother the news. Her mother gave her a big hug. "I knew you could do it," she said.

For the next two weeks

the little girl continued to practice.

The big day arrived. The little girl was excited and a bit nervous. After supper she went to her room to get dressed. She put on a pink tutu and pink ballet shoes, and around her neck she wore the silver slippers. Her mother tied her hair with a satin bow.

That night the school was aglow with lights when the little girl and her mother arrived. The little girl had never seen the school lit up like that.

All the ballerinas were in a flutter backstage. Most of them were already in their costumes and putting on their makeup. The little girl's mother helped her redden her lips and put pink on her cheeks. Looking in the mirror, she thought she looked quite like a ballerina. But she certainly didn't feel like one. "What if I miss a step? What if I trip on the stage? What if I can't do it?" the little girl thought to herself.

Now the little girl heard strains of music coming from below the stage. The performance was about to begin.

It was then that something unexpected happened.

While still in the wings, the little girl had a chance to look out at the audience. She became frightened. "How can I dance in front of all those people?" she thought. "I know I have dreamed about dancing on stage but I didn't think I would feel so nervous."

Then she remembered the silver slippers and what her mother had said. "These *are* special slippers," she thought. "When I see them I remember what I want to do. I *do* want to be the prima ballerina. I have worked hard and practiced. I have danced all the steps before. Many times before. And I can do it again."

Just then the piano sounded her entrance. The little girl took a deep breath and began to dance out onto the stage. She started a little shakily, but with each twirl and spin she became more confident. What's more, she never missed a step.

The curtain fell and applause filled the auditorium.

After the performance the teacher came up to the stage and presented the little girl with a bouquet of red roses. "For the most improved ballerina, who became the *star* ballerina," she said. The audience cheered, especially the little girl's mother.

From then on, the little girl wore the silver slippers every time she practiced. And on the days when she was learning a new step or one that was especially difficult, she would practice harder.

And it was true. The silver slippers were special. For they reminded her of what she really wanted—which was to dance her *very best.*